The

Adventures

Of

Fifi

By

Rosie Dooner

It was a lovely Spring day, the snow had finally cleared from the back garden, the only thing left was the remains of the snowman Bobby and Billy had built.

Betty was looking out of the window then said ` Who

fancies a trip out today?`

Bobby and Billy jumped in the air and squealed with excitement `Yaye.`

Fifi started to jump up and down when she watched the boys do it.

The family all laughed out loud because Fifi jumped up and down and round and round,she got a bit carried away with all her excitement.

Bert stopped
laughing then he
said ` I have a good

idea, lets go and drive too North Wales and check on our caravan after the winter frost.

I have some flower pots and plant bulbs which will be ready to plant for the summer flowers.

`Brilliant.` Bobby and Billy both said at the same time....

First Fifi ran after the boys, then she ran in the kitchen after Betty, then finally she followed Bert into the garage,

where he was
picking out plant

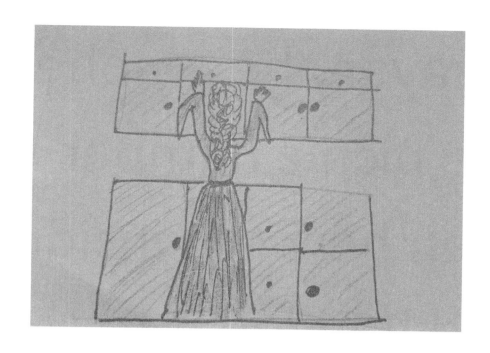

pots and a bag of
flower bulbs ready
to take to the

caravan, he grabbed the picnic hamper then he went inside and handed it to Betty who had made up a picnic for when they got to the caravan.

Once everything was ready Bert loaded up his car.

Fifi had her new coat and harness on for her lead. She loved being in the car and out with her family.

After a couple of hours they had reached their

destination and was parked up outside their caravan.

Their were a lot of families with the same idea, checking out their caravans.

Betty opened the door and started to unpack tins of food

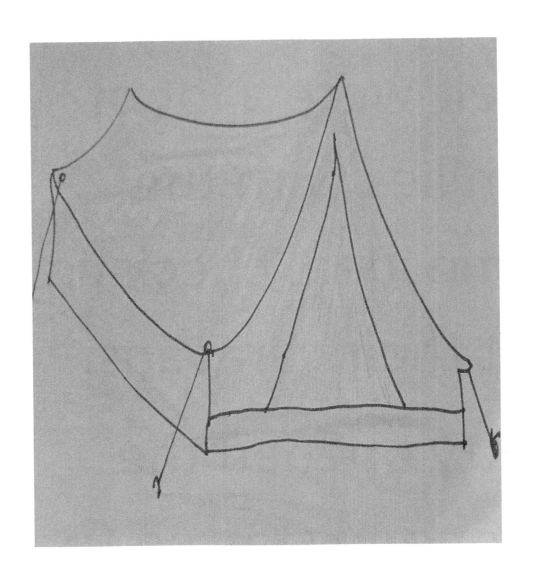

to put in her kitchen units, then she decided she wanted to spring clean the whole caravan so she cleared everyone out; including Fifi.

The boys were happy
they ran to the
swings, they saw

their friends playing there when they arrived....

Fifi ran after the boys down to the

park, after she had checked that Bert had eaten all his sweets.

Fifi watched as Billy and Bobby ran too

the ice-cream man first, they had an ice-cream then sat on the swings and ate them.

Fifi liked ice-cream. She looked about and saw the ice-cream man. He was very busy their

was a big line full of children just waiting too be served.

Fifi sat next to the children, she was waiting for the man to notice her sitting down like a good girl.

All the boys and girls had been served

they all went off to play on the swings at the park.

Finally the ice-cream man noticed Fifi. He started to get out of his van.... Fifi could see he had something in his hand so she went over to him expecting ice-cream...when he put it on the ground she went and sniffed it.. It was not ice cream, it was a bowl of fresh water. Which she drank any way it was a long car journey without a drink.

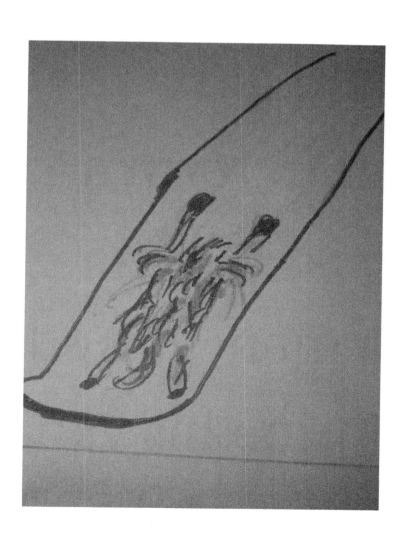

By now a lot more boys and girls started to form a queue so the ice-cream man walked back inside his van, only this time he forgot to shut the back door. He was busy serving his customers which gave Fifi a chance to sneak in through the door...

Fifi sniffed round all the boxes that she

could see until she found one opened...

Meanwhile back at the caravan Betty had shouted Bert,

Bobby and Billy to come back for some food.

Bobby and Billy ran from the park laughing. Bert came from inside the awning where he had been planting up flower pots. Betty had spent all her time cleaning, it smelt lovely and fresh. They all sat in the awning as Betty did not want one crumb on her clean floor.

They all sat eating and chatting away

suddenly Betty asked where Fifi was?

`She was not with me.` Bert said

`She came with us to the park, but their is a new fence round

the swings now so
she could not come
inside with us she sat
and watched us`

Bobby looked anxious `I never saw her when we ran back.`

Betty stood up and went outside looking about, their were no roads so she was safe that way she thought... Then she spotted the

ice-cream man.
Smiling she said ` I

think I might know where she is.

Betty walked over to the ice-cram van at the same time shouting `FIFI!!!`

She walked over to the counter and

asked the man if she had seen her dog, she had already been asking the rest of the people.

`Yes I saw her she was sitting over

there like a good girl,
so I came out and

gave her some water.

I got very busy after
that so came back

here... Oh look; that is a first, I have forgot to close the door behind me.` just as he went to shut his door he

heard a rustling sound.

`Did she drink any of the water?`

`Yes she did, she was thirsty.`

`hmmmm!` was the only sound coming from Betty.The ice-cream man

finished serving another customer.

`Oh Fifi where are you.` she said one more time...

Then she too heard
the rustling sound.
The next thing the
back door was open
and the man wave

Betty too come inside, then he

pointed to a box on the floor.

The ice-cream man pulled the box out lifted the lid..

They both laughed out loud at what they both saw.

Fifi was lying down in the box covered in broken wafer cones and chocolate flakes, not forgetting hundred and thousands sprinkles.

`It is okay lady, I use this as my bin, it was only going in the

food waste when I got back to the factory.`

They both laughed out loud one more time.

Fifi had only climbed into the box and started too eat what she could.

Fifi did not look happy at all.

`I think she has been very greedy and scoffed what she could, she might be

ill.` the ice-cream
man said with a sad
face.`i am very sorry
about all this. Do I

owe you money for
what she ate?`

`No no just take her away from here hygiene and all that.`

Betty picked Fifi up and carried her back to the caravan where she lay in her basket not moving an inch. Betty told

her family what Fifi had got up too, which of course they did laugh.

`I think I will put the plastic cover on the car seat on the way home incase she is sick, which I hope

she wont be,naughty
Fifi` Bert replied.

Fifi was sorry she scoffed stuff from the box...

Fifi did feel sick...

On the way back home she lay and slept most of the

way on a plastic sheet..

When they all arrived home Fifi went straight into her basket and slept...

I do not think she will be in a rush for

ice-cream next time.....

The End

Printed in Great Britain
by Amazon